I Spy I...

Written by Mal Peet and Elspeth Graham
Illustrated by Bernard Adnet

○ Collins

"I'm hungry," buzzed the fly.
"I need some food."
The fly buzzed off to look for food.

The fly buzzed up into the sky.
He looked around.
"I spy the park," buzzed the fly.
"I will look for food in the park."

"I'm hungry," buzzed the fly.
"And I spy a bun."
The fly buzzed off towards the bun.

The duck had already seen the bun.
The duck flapped his wings.
"Quack! Quack!"
The duck snapped at the bun with his beak.
"Oh, no," buzzed the fly and buzzed off.

"I'm still hungry," buzzed the fly.
"And I spy apples on a tree."
The fly dived for the apples.

The fly landed on an apple.
Next to the apple was a big spider's web.
The web shook. A big spider scuttled out.
"Help!" buzzed the fly and buzzed off.

"I'm very hungry now," buzzed the fly. "And I spy a lolly." The fly buzzed off for the lolly.

A dog was sniffing on the ground.
"Woof! Woof!"
Just as the fly reached the lolly,
the dog licked it up.
"I'm off," buzzed the fly and zoomed off.

"I'm really hungry now," buzzed the fly.
"And I spy chips in a rubbish bin."
The fly flew for the chips.

A dark shadow fell over him.
A gull landed on the bin. It had
a sharp, yellow beak.
Peck, peck.
"Time to go," buzzed the fly and buzzed off.

"I'm very, very hungry now," said the fly.
"And I spy a big cake."
The fly took off for the cake.

THWACK!
The fly banged into the window.
It was closed.

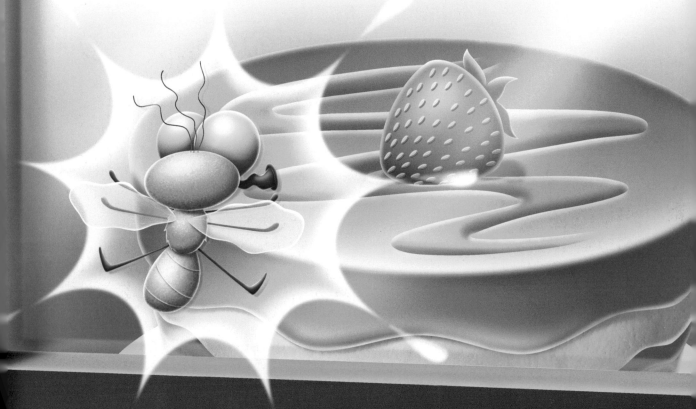

"Ouch!" buzzed the fly. "I don't feel
hungry now."
The fly buzzed off home.

I spy ...

14

15

Ideas for reading

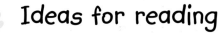

Written by Clare Dowdall BA(Ed), MA(Ed)
Lecturer and Primary Literacy Consultant

Learning objectives: read more challenging texts; read aloud with some variety in pace and emphasis; attempt to read more complex words using phonic knowledge; recognise alternative ways of pronouncing graphemes already taught; identify the constituent parts of two and three syllable words to support the use of phonics knowledge and skills; recognise automatically an increasing number of familiar high frequency words; identify the main events and characters in stories

Curriculum links: Science: Ourselves; Science: Health and growth

Focus phonemes: y, oo, zz, ea, i-e

Fast words: the, was, to, he, some

Word count: 282

Getting started

- Using flash cards, revise the fast words and check that children can recognise them.

- Read the title and blurb aloud together. Discuss what children know about flies and what the fly in the story might like to eat.

- Revise the focus phonemes *y*, *zz* and *oo* using whiteboards. Ask children to suggest words that contain these phonemes/graphemes and model writing them.

- Discuss strategies that can be used to read two syllable words. Model how to look for familiar word endings and to break words into constituent syllables.

Reading and responding

- Read pp2–3 with the children, modelling using an expressive voice for the fly.

- Ask the children to read from beginning to end, taking time to look at the pictures and use decoding skills to help them read and make meaning.